Robert M...

...ooks have so...

...orld, and he ...the bes...

...He has won...

... luding the...

...ward. For m...

Henderson's Boys to reluctant readers, because it never fails!' Cat, children's librarian

'My son could never see the point of reading a book until he read The Recruit. I want to thank you from the bottom of my heart for igniting the fire.' Donna

Also by Robert Muchamore

ROCK WAR

THE AUDITION

Robert Muchamore

h

Hodder
Children's
Books

A division of Hachette Children's Books

A Catalogue record for this book is available from the British Library

UK ISBN 978 1 444 92053 6
Export ISBN 978 1 444 92058 1

Typeset in Goudy by Avon DataSet Ltd,
Bidford-on-Avon, Warwickshire

Printed and bound in Great Britain by
CPI Group (UK) Ltd, Croydon, CR0 4YY

The paper and board used in this paperback by Hodder Children's
Books are natural recyclable products made from wood grown in
sustainable forests. The manufacturing processes conform to the
environmental regulations of the country of origin.

Hodder Children's Books
A division of Hachette Children's Books
338 Euston Road, London NW1 3BH
An Hachette UK company

www.hachette.co.uk

1. Lies, Damned Lies . . .

Sadie squatted down beside a wheelchair, a prehistoric school laptop casting a greenish hue on her cheeks. The year nine had broad shoulders, tatty walking boots, black school trousers and hair cropped short. She'd been called a lesbian so many times that it washed right over her.

'What you looking at?' Sadie asked.

Noah pushed his right wheel back a touch, so that he was facing her. 'Did you see that survey?'

Sadie took half a second to realise Noah's

words had nothing to do with the website on the laptop screen. 'What survey?'

'Scientists got this guy to go around a shopping mall. He had to strike up conversations with a hundred random women and try to get their phone number to set up a date.'

'Is this, like, a joke?' Sadie interrupted.

Noah tutted. 'I heard it on the radio, let me *finish* . . . So the first time the guy dresses in a smart business suit. He goes to the mall, chats up a hundred women and twelve of them give him their mobile numbers. The next day, he does the exact same thing, only he's dressed like a rugby dude, wearing a tracksuit and carrying a sports bag. He gets seventeen numbers. On the third and final day, he dresses up like a rock star and carries a guitar case. How many babes do you reckon give him their number?'

'How should I know?' Sadie says.

Noah cracked a big smile. 'Forty god-damned three! That's close to half, just hitting on random women in a shopping mall.'

'So what's your point?'

Noah opened his mouth wide, as if Sadie was an idiot. 'Chicks dig musicians. The way I figure it, losing my legs in a car crash is a major disadvantage when it comes to getting off with girls. But playing guitar pushes me back up to at least average.'

A pause in the conversation gave Sadie a chance to see what Noah had up on the laptop screen. She read some of it aloud in a mocking voice.

'*Ragecola dot com is proud to sponsor Rock War, a major new TV talent show for bands whose members are aged between twelve and seventeen . . . Would you like to spend your summer holidays at the Rock War Academy? Twelve bands will be picked from around the UK, blah, blah blah . . . Six weeks living on a luxurious country estate, having your skills honed by real-life rock stars and music industry pros. After that you'll need everything you've learned as your band faces eight weeks of musical challenges, live in front of a TV audience of millions.'*

When Sadie stopped reading, Noah read some more in a much more enthusiastic tone. *'One or two bands voted off each week . . . Winning band will receive a recording deal worth over half a million pounds and a chance to spend Christmas on a beautiful Caribbean island, recording tracks for your first album . . . To begin your shot at stardom, create a band profile and upload pictures, videos and demos of your band. The best bands will be invited to one of six auditions, held in Belfast, Cardiff, Edinburgh, London, Manchester or Newcastle.'*

Sadie shrugged and sucked a little air through her teeth. 'I was into those shows when I was like nine, but they're all exactly the same.'

Noah shook his head. 'I never watched all that X-Factor rubbish in the first place. But who's talking about watching it? I'm talking about being *in* the show.'

As Noah said this, he opened another tab

in the web browser. 'I started a band profile for the Unicorns.'

Sadie was moderately impressed when she saw the work Noah had put into the Unicorns' profile on the Rock War website. He'd made and uploaded a band logo, plus some videos the three-strong band had made while jamming the previous summer, and he'd written a short biography for each member.

Sadie read the profile Noah had written about her: *A tomboy with attitude, Sadie writes mean lyrics, plays drums or guitar. She really likes custard cream biscuits and has been known to eat them till she pukes.*

'So that's what you think of me,' Sadie said, half smiling. 'But even leaving aside the fact that twenty bazillion bands are going to try and enter this thing, the Unicorns broke up.'

'We never officially broke up,' Noah said. 'We just haven't practised for a while . . .'

'For a year,' Sadie said. 'Chris doesn't

give a damn about music since Ellie stole his heart.'

'Those two are so in love it makes me gag,' Noah said. 'But if I upload the profile and we get a shot at the Belfast audition, I reckon we can get him back in the band.'

'I wouldn't bet on it,' Sadie said, as she shook her head. 'Ellie's dead possessive. Remember Easter hols when Chris was playing your Scalextric? She was texting him the whole time saying she was lonely and he left after barely an hour.'

'You're right about there being loads of entries,' Noah said. 'Miss McGowan put a Rock War poster on the music-room noticeboard. She said there's at least four bands entering just from this school. But on the other hand, it doesn't cost anything, except an hour writing some blurb about the band and uploading a few files.'

'Whatever makes you happy, mate,' Sadie said dismissively, as she glanced at her watch. 'I've got that detention for not doing my

RS homework. You gonna stick around till I'm done?'

Noah shook his head. 'Profile's finished. I'm just gonna hit the upload button and roll out of here.'

'It's only half an hour,' Sadie said. 'You sure you'll be all right on the bus?'

'I managed on my own for a week when you went on the geography trip.'

'Right,' Sadie said, a touch uneasily. 'There shouldn't be too many kids crowding around the bus stop by the time you get there. You want me to come round at half sevenish and we can do that history assignment?'

'Nah, my dad's taking me to archery tonight.'

'Tomorrow at the bus stop, then?'

'Laters,' Noah said, raising one arm into a quick wave as his best friend headed out.

After a thoughtful glance around his deserted form room, Noah turned back to the laptop. He started reading through the stuff he'd written for the Rock War profile, but he'd already checked it all twice and he decided it was as good as he could make it.

Noah slid a chewed fingernail down the trackpad until the mouse hovered over the UPLOAD AND ACTIVATE BAND PROFILE button. He hesitated, thinking about Sadie's whole, *it's cheesy, pointless and the Unicorns are not even a band any more* vibe. But entering Rock War was free and he'd spent an entire form lesson making up the profile.

The screen froze just long enough for Noah to think he'd not clicked properly. Then a pop-up box with the Rock War logo appeared, and a message beneath it.

Error!

Your data has been uploaded and saved, but your band profile cannot go live because: %&Error21 Your Rock War profile is incomplete. You must enter details for all four band members.

Noah swore, then he muttered under his breath, 'The Unicorns are a three-piece band, you stupid asswipe machine.'

After clicking again and getting the same error, Noah went back to the profile. His first thought was to trick the computer by sticking a few dots in the boxes for the fourth band member and trying to submit for a third time. But he decided to go back to the site's main page and check the entry FAQs.

Noah thought he'd read them all before starting work on the band profile, but somehow he'd missed the third question:

What if my band has more or fewer than four members?

We're very sorry, but due to the nature of the tasks and accommodation provided during the training camp phase of Rock War, the competition is only open to bands with four members.

'Bloody hell!' Noah moaned, as he pounded the desk hard enough to make the laptop jolt.

He tried to think his way out of the problem, but it would be a stretch just to get Chris out of Ellie's arms to attend an audition. There was no way he'd be able to recruit a new band member, rehearse, change all the band pictures and make new demos in the three days left before the cut-off date for profile uploads.

Noah felt gutted as he snapped the laptop lid down and started wheeling himself towards the classroom door. It seemed that some things just weren't meant to be.

2. Alpha Pups

Nobody ever gave Noah room in the crowded school corridors, so it was always a relief to roll out between the swing doors at morning break. He liked having space and fresh air, even though it was drizzling.

Being in a wheelchair bestowed a few perks. One was being allowed to skip the lunch line, another was the disabled ramp just left of the school's front entrance. It hadn't been built right, so going up the steep slope was a workout, but freewheeling down a total hoot.

Noah aligned his chair at the top, then fully released his brake. The chair juddered as it picked up speed and he made a low humming sound, because he liked the way the vibrations made his voice judder.

In wet weather, the biggest thrill came at the bottom, where Noah's slim black tyres would aquaplane for a couple of metres. You had to brake just right: too hard and you'd get thrown out of the chair, too late and you'd run off the pavement and have to ask someone to pull your front wheels out of the muddy gutter.

After using the ramp three or four times a day since he was in year seven, Noah was an expert. But today, he got two thirds of the way down and saw Fergal Doolan standing at the bottom.

'Mind out my way!' Noah shouted urgently.

Fergal saw what was coming too late. He managed half a step back, but the wheelchair hit his knee and ankle at full pelt. Noah got thrown sideways in the chair, and had a heart-in-mouth moment where he thought he was going head first into the pavement.

Throwing his torso to one side rebalanced the chair, but Fergal wasn't so lucky. After a few hops, clutching ripped school trousers over a skinned knee, he clattered into a wire bin and ended up blotting a puddle with his butt.

'I'm gonna rip your head off,' Fergal shouted, as he grabbed the bin to stand up. 'Why didn't you stop?'

There were plenty of idiots at Noah's school, but Fergal belonged to an elite group of people whom he actively hated. Noah could tolerate kids who thought it was funny to drop crisps and orange peel down the back of your wheelchair, kids who rolled you into dark cupboards and shut the door, and kids who insisted on turfing you out so they could take your chair for a ride.

Fergal was worse, because as well as being a dick, he packed the kind of torso that you might see modelling on a three-pack of underwear, and had a blue-eyed-square-jawed thing going on that set all the girls' hearts aflutter. If a fat spotty kid took liberties you could tell them to piss off, but when it was Fergal and his clique, you either laughed along with their 'joke' or got accused of being uncool.

'You're a madman,' Fergal yelled, as he found his feet, flipped his blonde fringe off his face, then reached around to peel sodden Calvin Kleins away from his butt cheeks.

Noah looked behind, hoping Sadie had caught up. She wouldn't beat Fergal in a fight, but she wouldn't stand for any nonsense either.

'It's a wheelchair, not a formula one car,' Noah yelled, hoping that a member of staff would hear before Fergal decided to tip his chair, or roll him into the shrubbery. 'I can't just stop dead.'

'My knee's bleeding.'

'Funniest thing I've seen all week,' a

stunning girl called Poppy said, beaming as she jogged up behind Fergal and thumped him on the back. 'Only a gormless ape like you would stand at the bottom waiting to get clonked.'

Fergal kept scowling, until Poppy went up on tiptoes and pecked his cheek. 'Kiss you better?' she said sweetly.

'You know how much hassle my mum gives me about my uniform getting wrecked,' Fergal moaned.

Noah felt jealous, seeing the big alpha-male getting fawned over by the third hottest girl in his year. He'd only ever snogged Sadie, and that was an experiment when they were in year seven and smuggled a bottle of caramel liqueur up to her room during a sleepover.

The fourth person on the scene was someone Noah thought was OK. Joe hung out with the year nine cool set, but he was one of the few who managed to combine it with behaving like a decent human being.

He was brilliant at art. He'd worked with Noah on scenery for a Christmas play, and even jammed on guitar in the practice rooms with him a couple of times.

'You just stood there, Fergal,' Joe said. 'You're such an unco.'

'It's only a wet arse,' Fergal said, smiling now as Poppy slid her palm across his lower back, until her arm hugged his waist.

'We came down here to find you,' Joe told Noah.

Noah realised it was weird seeing Poppy and Fergal in this part of the school. Misfits like him and Sadie hung out below the school's main entrance, precisely because kids like Fergal held the turf around the all-weather pitches on the opposite side of the building.

'Me, why?'' Noah asked, as he looked behind again, still hoping that Sadie would arrive to cover his back. 'What do you want me for?'

Joe made an air guitar as he spoke. 'You

play really good. Angle Grinder needs a bass player, pronto.'

Noah looked confused. 'Are you playing a gig or something?'

'Have you seen the poster in the music rooms for that Rock War TV show?' Poppy asked.

Noah tried to play it cool. 'I might have glanced at it,' he said vaguely. 'But doesn't that year ten dude, Lorcan, play bass with you guys?'

Poppy nodded. 'Lorcan's parents are divorced, so he has to spend the summer in Istanbul with his dad.'

'Which rules him out of Rock War,' Joe added. 'And you're the only other decent guitar player we know.'

Fergal couldn't resist having a dig. 'Obviously you'll have to sit out of sight, behind my drum kit.'

Joe sounded angry. 'Stop being a tit, Fungal. We *need* this guy.'

Noah enjoyed saying that he didn't care

about the likes of Poppy and Joe, but he was flattered by their attention.

'It's been a while since I've played with a band,' Noah said. 'But I guess it could be fun.'

'Plan is to practise tonight,' Joe said. 'And we want something that really stands out on our Rock War profile. I've borrowed a video camera off my uncle. We're gonna shoot a little promo vid tomorrow. I'll edit it together Sunday and upload our profile just before the deadline.'

'So are you in or what?' Poppy asked, giving Noah a smile.

'What the hell,' Noah said, unable to stifle his grin any longer. 'Where do I sign?'

3. I Swear To Good You Are God At This

The bell had gone for the end of school. Noah's form-room doorway was a crush of black blazers and the corridor beyond churned with kids set free.

'Stop shoving,' Noah's form tutor, Mr Hammond, yelled.

Noah always waited for the crush to die down before wheeling out. Sadie sat alongside with her legs swinging off a desk, eyes focused on the floor tiles.

'You want me to walk to the music block

with you?' she asked sourly.

'What's your problem?' Noah asked.

'Who says I have a problem?'

Noah tutted. 'You've barely spoken since I said I was going to practise with Angle Grinder. You're down on Rock War, but why shouldn't I take my chance?'

Sadie shook her head. 'It's not about Rock War, it's about *those* people.'

'Joe's OK.'

'When he's alone,' Sadie admitted. 'But he can be just as much of an arse as Fergal when he's with that crowd.'

'Can't I make friends with other people?' Noah asked.

'It's so not about that,' Sadie said. 'How many times have you told me that you hate that whole crew? But Poppy and Fergal give you a wink and smile and you're jumping through hoops for them, like a dog on a lead.'

'How can a dog on a lead jump through hoops?'

'You know what I mean.'

'OK you two,' Mr Hammond said, jangling a set of keys. 'Haven't you got homes to go to?'

The crowd in the hallway had thinned and Noah wheeled out.

'So what about the history project?' Sadie asked. 'Shall I come round yours tomorrow?'

'That's when we're shooting the video. I'm free Sunday.'

Sadie was free, but she didn't want Noah to think that she had nothing else going on.

'Sunday's this whole big family thing,' she lied. 'Going over to my aunt's place in Bangor. So do you want me to walk to the music room with you or not?'

'I'll make my own way,' Noah said, as the pair reached a T-junction. 'I need to go right for the lift.'

'See you Monday then, I guess,' Sadie said. She turned left and took a few steps, then turned and looked at the back of Noah's chair. 'I hope the rehearsal goes well,

Noah,' she yelled. 'Just don't let Fergal treat you like crap.'

'I'm a big boy,' Noah called back, a touch irritably.

After going down in the lift and a long roll across the school's deserted ground floor, Noah reached a windowless practice room. The first thing to catch his eye was Poppy. She'd had PE last lesson, and looked dead sexy, standing at her keyboard in Nikes and thigh-hugging shorts.

'Hey, hey, everyone,' Fergal said, as he did a little de-dum-dum and cymbal crash on his drum kit. 'It's Noah the turd!'

Poppy threw something. It skimmed Fergal's hair and pelted a whiteboard printed with music staves.

'What did I tell you?' Poppy warned.

As Noah tried to ignore Fergal, he got a more friendly greeting from Joe, then bumped fists with an olive-skinned kid with a mass of dark curls.

'I'm Lorcan,' the kid said. 'You're gonna

be playing my parts, so I'll show you the ropes.'

'Cool,' Noah said. He was startled by Joe tossing a bottle of water his way, but recovered in time to pick it out of the air.

'Nice catch,' Joe said. 'You'll need that. We have to keep the door closed and it gets well stuffy once there's a few bodies in here.'

Lorcan had his guitar set up. 'We're starting with "Seven Nation Army", do you know it?'

Noah smiled, feeling like he'd passed some kind of test as he wheeled up to a music stand. 'The White Stripes. I've never played it, but I know roughly how it goes.'

'Nice easy one to start with,' Lorcan said, giving a little demo before handing his guitar down to Noah. 'You come in the same time as Poppy's drums. Is that comfortable?'

Noah played with the guitar tucked under his left arm and resting in his lap, so Lorcan took the neck strap off to stop it getting tangled.

'Nobody screw up,' Fergal yelled, before making a three count with his drumsticks.

Joe began playing the song's opening riff. He was average at best and Noah could have done better after an hour's practice. But Fergal was a solid drummer, and Poppy's voice had an earthy, slightly scratchy tone that suited the White Stripes' song perfectly.

Noah hit a bum note as he cut in with the unfamiliar bass, but after that he was fine. The music made him feel like he belonged, and although he was only feeling his way with the song, and he found playing bass guitar monotonous, a huge smile erupted across his face when Lorcan gave him two thumbs up.

Things got a little ragged by the time the song entered its final minute, but when 'Seven Nation Army' ground to a halt, Joe laughed and Poppy came out from behind her keyboard and gave Noah's shoulder a squeeze.

'Not bad for a first stab,' Poppy said cheerfully. 'Not bad at all.'

*

'No, I didn't get detention,' Noah told his mum when she called to ask why he wasn't home. 'It's a music thing, I'll explain later . . . No worries, I'll stick it in the microwave . . . Yeah, Mum. I'll probably be fine, but of course I'll call if I need you to pick me up.'

Noah felt embarrassed as he dropped his phone into the pocket of his white school shirt, but the other members of Angle Grinder had barely even noticed. Poppy was folding up her keyboard stand, while Joe unplugged the guitar amps.

'Good rehearsal,' Poppy said. 'Anyone for Starbucks?'

Lorcan and Fergal had a cash-in-hand job at the garden centre where Lorcan's dad worked, so it was just Poppy, Joe and Noah who took a ten-minute stroll to the high street. Noah had a thing about being independent and didn't like people pushing his chair, but he let Poppy do it because she was hot, and she kept telling him how great he'd done for a first rehearsal.

Noah's parents said Starbucks was stupidly expensive, and Sadie reckoned it was a big evil corporation, so he'd never actually been in one before. He tried to act like it wasn't a new experience, and he got around not knowing what to order by having the same thing as Joe.

Joe watched rain pelting the front windows as Noah picked up his Grande Latte and took a slightly suspicious sip. It tasted more of milk than anything, which was good because coffee didn't do much for him.

'I hope the weather's better for the video shoot tomorrow,' Joe said.

Noah struggled to find something to say. 'It's cool that your uncle's letting you borrow his camcorder.'

'Can't you just shoot on a mobile phone?' Poppy asked.

'You can, but it would suck,' Joe explained. 'My uncle Toby's got a camera with interchangeable lenses and stuff. And he's got a tripod and a bag stuffed with gear. I'm OK with the software, but he said he's free to help me do the edit and sound mix if I need him to.'

'Is he a pro?' Noah asked.

Joe shook his head. 'Toby works for Waitrose. But I've made a few short films with him and I wanna do filmmaking when I go to uni.'

'I thought you'd do art,' Poppy said, as she sucked iced mocha through a straw. 'You're so good at it.'

Noah smirked. 'Maybe we'll win Rock War, and be megastars before we even get to uni.'

Poppy and Joe both laughed, which gave Noah a kind of warm glowy feeling. Joe said something, but Noah missed it because his phone chimed.

'Probably my mum again,' Noah said

warily. But it was a text from Sadie.

Hope rehearsals going well, S.

Poppy leaned over nosily and read the message. 'It's cool the way you and Sadie do everything together.'

Joe nodded. 'I was at primary with Sadie and Noah. I always remember them being together. Even way back in Reception.'

Noah liked the compliments, but was thrown off kilter by the idea that a goddess like Poppy thought something about him was cool.

'What about Fergal?' Noah asked. 'You must be close. He's your boyfriend, isn't he?'

Poppy smirked, then wagged a finger. 'Let me tell you something, in confidence, OK? Fergal can be sweet sometimes, and he's like, oh-my-god FIT! But we've been going steady for three months and I can't remember a single decent conversation.'

'So dump him,' Joe said. 'His humongous ego could do with some denting.'

'He's arm candy,' Poppy said, grinning

mischievously. 'I'm fourteen. It's not like I'm looking for a husband, is it?'

Noah smiled, but on the inside he felt out of place. He'd never had a girlfriend, so Joe and Poppy's casual talk about relationships made them seem way more sophisticated than him.

'So,' Poppy said, as she grabbed her half-drunk drink and stood up. 'I'm desperate to shower and get out of this dorky PE kit.'

'Want me to join you in the shower?' Joe asked.

Poppy gave him an up-yours gesture. 'See you both at the shoot tomorrow.'

'I'll send you a text with the details,' Joe said. 'I'd better make a move as well. Do you know your way home from here, Noah?'

Noah nodded. 'Bus right outside takes me home.'

Once Poppy and Joe were gone, Noah pulled his phone back out and stared at the text from Sadie, feeling guilty that he'd been off having fun with other people.

Rehearsal = great!!! Maybe I can come around yours to do homework after the shoot 2moro.

Sadie replied almost instantly.

Perhaps Sunday. Apparently the family thing with my auntie has been cancelled.

4. Lights, Camel, Action . . .

Noah sat in their smartly fitted kitchen while his mum emptied the dishwasher.

'I'm just meeting some kids from school, we're gonna make a video.'

Noah's mum got a thin-lipped beady-eyed look when she didn't like something. 'It's just that I don't know any of these kids, and you've got no idea how long you're going to be.'

'I'm not a baby. I'm fourteen!'

'If I could just speak to one of their parents, or something.'

'Mum, NO!' Noah protested. 'I'm trying to make some new friends. Have you any idea how embarrassing it'll be if I have to ring one of them up and ask if you can speak to their parents?'

'What if there's no mobile phone signal?'

'It's the local park, not the Kalahari Desert.'

Noah's mum was still grumpy as they drove four miles out to Forest Park on the edge of Belfast. As the people carrier pulled up, Joe and Poppy were at the park gates, along with two hefty sports bags, a big video tripod and a guy who looked about twenty.

'Who's he?' Noah's mum asked suspiciously.

'It's probably Satan,' Noah said, as he pressed the button to open a sliding side door and began lifting himself into his wheelchair. 'I expect he'll hack me to pieces with an axe the second you drive off.'

'Maybe I'll just go over and say hello,' she said, as Noah lined himself up with the motorised ramp growing out the side of the vehicle.

'Maybe I'll just put rat poison in the next cup of tea I make you,' Noah said, as he wheeled off. 'Love you, Mum, see you later.'

Noah felt bad being rude when his mum did so much for him, but was also mightily relieved that she drove off as soon as the sliding door closed.

'My uncle, Toby,' Joe said, by way of introduction.

'Hey,' Noah said, as he studied the pencil-thin man, dressed in aviator sunglasses, a 1970s style brown leather jacket and skinny jeans. 'I thought you'd be older.'

'My ma's like, fifteen years older than Toby,' Joe explained. 'So he's more like a big brother than an uncle.'

Noah was surprised to find Toby handing him a snazzy business card which read, *Toby Jugg, Viral Marketing Specialist*.

'I thought you worked for Waitrose,' Noah said.

'Delivering groceries pays the bills right now,' Toby said, sounding a touch offended. 'But I've got my fingers in lots of pies. One of my YouTube videos has over 800,000 hits.'

'Cool,' Noah said, as he saw the YouTube address on the back of the business card. 'I'll take a peek at your website next time I'm online.'

'Toby's off work today,' Joe explained. 'He knows the camera equipment better than me.'

'And I pointed out that it's easier to do shots of the whole band if there's someone standing behind the camera,' Toby added.

'So where's Fergal?' Noah asked.

'He'll be late for his own funeral,' Poppy said.

It spat with rain as they waited. Toby and Joe crouched over the equipment bags and started fitting waterproof housings to a swanky-looking video camera.

'Hey, losers,' Fergal said, as he came out

from the passenger seat of his dad's work van.

Joe introduced Toby, and Fergal sneered at his business card before eyeballing him. 'You look like a stiff breeze would flatten you.'

Then Fergal stepped up to Poppy, grabbed her arse tightly with one hand and gave her an aggressive kiss, sticking his tongue deep into her mouth. It was like Fergal was marking his territory in front of the other males.

Poppy looked a bit shocked as they broke apart. But Fergal gave her a smile and raised one eyebrow before saying, 'Morning, beautiful.'

Poppy seemed to like Fergal's cheek, and lifted one leg off the ground as they exchanged a more gentle kiss. She looked amazing in a tiny black skirt and tight T-shirt. Fergal seemed pleased with himself after the snog and Noah hated him more than ever.

'So we're just gonna do a variety of shots,'

Toby explained, as he slung one of the equipment bags over his shoulder and started leading the group towards a wooded area a few hundred metres inside the park. 'In the trees, by the lake, up the top of the hill with a view over the city. I don't want it to be too po-faced. I've got some cheesy props, like an inflatable beach ball, bucket and spade. Then I'll edit it together with that recording of you guys playing Nine Inch Nails' "Sunspots".'

'Sounds crap,' Fergal said. 'Why can't we do a proper hardcore rock video? Just the three of us bashing our instruments with some moody lighting, and Noah with a paper bag over his head.'

Toby made a deep sigh, and talked down to Fergal. 'Have you looked at the profiles on Rockwar dot com? There's already a hundred videos of spotty kids pretending to be Guns n' Roses up there. If you want a profile that's gonna land an audition, you've got to make something that stands out.'

Poppy didn't like Fergal's general meanness and gave him a dig in the ribs. 'Stop busting balls, or I'll bust yours,' she warned.

Fergal loved playing the bad boy. He walked backwards for a few steps, facing Noah while he started singing, 'Loser, loser, loser . . . You don't mind, do you mate?'

Noah felt his lips tighten, and suspected that his expression was exactly like the one his mum got when she was angry. But he sucked up the insult and kept his mouth shut.

*

The video began as Joe's project, but it was Toby's equipment and he took charge once they started shooting. Angle Grinder's four members got filmed doing all kinds of random stuff: chasing between and jumping out of trees, lobbing stones in the lake. Noah got soaked during a shot where Toby asked him to wheel himself as fast as possible through an ankle-deep pool, much to the ire of several ducks and their offspring.

But while some stuff was fun, mostly Angle Grinder were just waiting around while Toby set up his video camera for the next shot. By 2 p.m. they were all bored and tired.

'How much loooooonger?' Fergal moaned, as he sat on slightly damp grass with Poppy using his stomach as a pillow.

'Just a few more shots,' Toby said, as he sat on a tree stump, playing back some of the footage he'd shot on his laptop, while Joe peered over his shoulder.

'You said that fourteen hours ago,' Poppy said. 'I'm so hungry I'm starting to feel faint.'

'We're getting great footage,' Joe said. 'The time we put in now will all be on show when I edit your video together.'

'I'm past caring,' Fergal said, as he stood up. 'The rest of yous can stay here all day if you want, but I'm out of here.'

Fergal put his hand out to haul Poppy out of the grass, and she accepted reluctantly.

'Sorry guys,' she said. 'I didn't get any breakfast.'

Noah wasn't desperate to leave, but he was a bit soggy and Poppy mentioning food made him realise that he was hungry too. Toby jogged towards Fergal and Poppy as they started walking away.

'How about just one more shot?' Toby begged. 'Ten minutes, max.'

Poppy stopped walking, holding Fergal's hand as if he was straining on a leash. 'What shot?' she asked.

'Wearing the head camera,' Toby explained. 'The footage is good, apart from Noah. It won't cut well, because he moves across the grass at a different speed to everyone else.'

'Can't you speed it up when you edit?' Joe asked.

Toby shook his head. 'You can, but it doesn't look smooth.'

'I went as fast as I could,' Noah said.

'Noah, you did great,' Toby said warmly.

'But can we just do one more shot with someone pushing the wheelchair, so the speed of the wheelchair shots will match the speed of the shots taken with you guys running. Then I'll review the footage and let you go.'

Fergal let go of Poppy's hand and smiled as he walked back. 'I'll push his chair.'

Noah looked alarmed. 'Maybe Joe should do it,' he blurted. 'He knows more about the camera and stuff.'

'I'm fastest,' Fergal said, cracking an evil grin. 'Get outta my way.'

Noah felt uneasy as Fergal gripped the fold-out handles on the back of his chair. Toby fitted a fresh battery and memory card to a tiny head cam, before attaching it to Noah's head with an elastic strap.

'Where do I go?' Fergal asked.

Toby shrugged. 'It doesn't really matter. It'll be cut so fast that you'll barely notice.'

Fergal gave Noah an unfriendly whack on the shoulder. 'Got your seatbelt on, saddo?'

'He doesn't have one,' Poppy noted.

'That's a pity,' Fergal said, as he put his body behind Noah's wheelchair and thrust forwards hard enough to make Noah think he was going to tip over backwards. 'Geronimo!'

Fergal set off, going slightly uphill along a concrete path. Noah used to enjoy letting his dad push him fast when he was little, but he trusted his dad not to let go.

After about a hundred metres, with Poppy giving chase and Joe and Toby moving more slowly with equipment bags slung over their backs, Fergal cut off the path into some long grass. Noah had a top-of-the-line chair with air suspension, but his back still jarred on the bumps and the spinning tyres sprayed water up his jeans.

'Doggy doos!' Fergal shouted, as he jerked the chair violently to avoid a brown pile glistening with bluebottles.

At the crest of the hill, Noah felt a blast of wind, and a few spots of rain. The shaking had made the camera slide down to the bridge of his nose, and he pushed it up as Poppy shouted a breathless, 'Be careful!'

Fergal had used all his strength to push the wheelchair up the hill, now he needed it to keep ahold as it picked up speed on a steep downwards slope towards a pond at the bottom. Noah kept one hand over his brake lever, but at this kind of speed he feared that the slightest touch would catapult him face first across the grass.

Noah's fears of landing in the drink subsided as they neared the bottom of the hill. The gradient relaxed and the chair slowed enough that Fergal was back to controlling the chair, instead of the chair dragging him.

The lakeside was muddy, making the front wheels dig in and Noah was almost thrown out once again. His hands gripped the armrests as Fergal drove along the lakeside, through puddles and gravel.

At one point they were centimetres from

the pond's edge. A huge dog scrambled off the hill on to the path in front of them, yelping as it spun and jumped out of their path. In shock, Fergal stumbled.

Noah felt the chair veering towards the lake and dabbed his left brake, altering his trajectory just enough to send himself freewheeling back on to the path, carving a plume of water as he shot through a large puddle.

Fergal would have gone in the water, but fortunately stumbled on to a wooden pontoon used by anglers. His weight made the floating structure tilt to one side, sending a little wave lapping across the slatted deck. A pair of anglers at the end of the pontoon glanced back in surprise, while a large man fishing closer to shore ran out of luck.

The angler had put up a nylon shelter to shield himself from the rain and Fergal hit it at full pelt. As spring-loaded tent poles buckled, Fergal hit the fisherman in the back, bundling him head first into the water.

As Noah wheeled to a genteel halt, the tent caught the wind and flew out over the lake, while Fergal wound up face down, with his face hanging over the pontoon's edge. The water was only waist deep and he found himself being grabbed at the throat by a giant, dripping angler.

'You little turd!' the angler roared. 'I'm gonna wring your neck!'

5. Fugite

The soggy angler was a beast. Fergal used all his strength to break the man's grasp, then felt a huge fist slam into his eye socket. Back on the path, Noah tried to wheel away, but his skinny tyres offered little grip on the mixture of mud and gravel.

'I saw that!' someone shouted.

As Fergal found his feet, and avenged the punch by booting the angler's Thermos flask and tackle box into the water, Noah looked around and saw a park keeper in a day-glo vest sprinting downhill towards them. Joe and Toby got to about twenty metres from water's edge, before deciding to leg it with the bags of delicate equipment thumping against their backs.

Fergal started running, with one of the dry anglers giving chase, and the dripping wet dude following up. Noah looked about, feeling abandoned.

Poppy's Converse skidded as she reached the path, but she stayed on her feet and grabbed the handles. She wasn't as strong as Fergal, but once Noah's chair had a bit of momentum she was belting along the lakeside, bare legs getting pelted by mud and gravel thrown up from the back wheels.

After a couple of hundred metres, Poppy turned on to a concrete path which led around the crest of the hill. Noah's chair wasn't great on grass or mud, but on a hard surface like concrete he could wheel himself faster than most people can run.

Wheelchair use had given Noah strong arms. He caught up with Joe and Toby after about five hundred metres, with Poppy about fifty metres back and getting short of breath.

Fergal had taken a steeper route towards the top of the hill, before turning back down towards the others. The two anglers chasing him couldn't handle the hill and wound up clutching their sides, but the park keeper was younger and faster.

As Noah led a charge towards a kiddies' playground and a park exit, the guy in the day-glo vest got within touching distance of Fergal and tried a rugby tackle. But rugby was Fergal's game. As the park keeper lunged, Fergal sidestepped. When the park keeper sprawled out half a step in front of him, Fergal couldn't resist treading on his outstretched hand.

The park keeper yelped and at first the pain just made him more determined to bring Fergal down. But by the time he got to running at full pelt again, Fergal had caught up with the others and the park keeper didn't fancy his chances taking on five teenagers.

Noah was wheeling through the park gates when the park keeper finally gave up. He stood with hands on hips, pointing furiously towards Fergal's back.

'You're all banned from this park,' he spat. 'I know your faces.'

Fergal gave a two-fingered salvo as he jogged through the park's main gates, then looked around at a narrow lane parked up with cars. 'Where the hell are we?'

Poppy already had her iPhone out, trying to check the GPS while keeping up a jog. 'I kind of know where we are,' she said breathlessly. 'I was here once for my primary school sports day. My mum brought her car, but I can remember kids waiting at a bus stop at the top of this road.'

'It better not take too long to arrive,' Joe said. 'If the cops turn up we're screwed.'

But Toby was older and wiser. 'What he did was dumb,' Toby said, pointing at Fergal.

'But knocking the guy in the water was an accident. Him grabbing you by the throat and socking you one, that was common assault. If he's dumb enough to call the cops, he'll be the one who ends up in the dock.'

Fergal cracked a smile. 'Toby, you're pretty smart for a skinny streak of piss. So why don't *we* call the cops?'

Toby shook his head. 'When I win the lotto, the first thing I'm gonna do is enrol Fergal in charm school.'

'You mean I got all out of breath for nothing?' Joe added.

Toby shook his head. 'We don't call the cops, because they'll question us for hours, probably confiscate my equipment and all the footage we shot as evidence. So let's just let sleeping dogs lie, and get out of here as fast as we can.'

*

Noah always pictured the cool kids living in great big ranch houses, like in some American TV show, with Mercs and BMWs clustered on the driveway. After a bus ride and a five-minute roll past grim pebble-dashed terraces with grilles over all the ground floor windows, Noah found himself in a hallway so narrow that his muddy wheels almost scraped both sides.

The living room in Poppy's house opened out on to a titchy back yard, stacked with faded ride-on toys and lines of little kids' clothes, strung out in spite of the drizzle. But if the ambience was lacking, the atmosphere was great.

Poppy's mum was out at work, but her older brother lived there with his girlfriend, Suzie, and their two little boys. The older boy was about six, and fascinated by Noah's wheelchair. He asked questions until he got told that it was rude. Suzie made tea and came out with a big pack of Jaffa Cakes. Noah ate four, even though they were cheapo supermarket brand, not the McVitie's ones he made his mum buy.

While Fergal sat in an armchair, holding

a bag of frozen sweetcorn over his eye to stop it swelling, they scoffed tea and biscuits and told Suzie about what had happened at the park. Now that they were safe, the story became a big adventure and everyone exaggerated their part.

'Noah's chair was like *that* close to going in the pond,' Poppy squealed, holding her thumb and forefinger a couple of centimetres apart. 'Oh my god!'

'Can you swim?' Suzie asked.

'Yeah,' Noah said. 'Though I'm not too fast without my fins strapped on.'

Joe seemed curious. 'So if you've got flippers for swimming, how come you can't use artificial legs?'

'I've got some crappy fake legs,' Noah explained. 'But they weigh a ton, so I prefer the chair. Once I stop growing I'm gonna get some titanium ones. They're computerised, so you balance automatically.'

'Why can't you get them now?' Poppy asked.

'Because they cost, like, twenty grand a pair and I'd need a new set every time I had a growth spurt.'

Toby smiled. 'If you had one big flipper, you'd look like a mermaid.'

'You'd need tits though,' Fergal said, which made Suzie's six-year-old bury his face and howl with laughter.

'Screw you guys,' Noah said, not minding because he kind of felt like a soldier, back from a dangerous mission with some new comrades. 'My mum's gonna freak when she sees the state of this chair, though.'

Suzie's boyfriend pointed out back. 'There's a hose out there. And your T-shirt's a state, but I can lend yous a clean one.'

So Noah climbed out of his chair on to the sofa. While Joe and Suzie's boyfriend hosed all the mud off his wheelchair, her younger son ran upstairs and came back with an armful of his dad's T-shirts.

'He only needs one,' Suzie said, as she took a pile of T-shirts out of her son's arms and gave him a kiss on the forehead. 'Looks like you've got a choice, Noah.'

Noah was chuffed, because he was able to pick a pale blue SuperDry shirt almost identical to one that he owned. Hopefully his mum wouldn't even notice.

'Whoah!' Poppy said, as Noah pulled his muddy T-shirt over his head. Noah thought he'd committed some horrible sin by pulling his shirt off, but when his head popped through the hole, he found Suzie and Poppy both smiling at him.

'What did I do?' he asked anxiously.

'Look at those pecs!' Poppy said. 'And those shoulders.'

'You're buff, Noah!' Suzie squealed.

Noah felt his face turn red, then redder as Poppy squeezed his bicep.

'Well obviously, your arms and shoulders develop more if you're pushing a wheelchair around. Plus I do archery, so I do exercises for that as well.'

'Are you any good?' Suzie asked.

'I've represented Northern Ireland, under eighteen.'

Fergal didn't like Noah getting the girls' attention. 'How hard is that though?' he sniped. 'I saw some of the Paralympics in 2012. There's like a billion categories in each event, so you're probably only competing against four other kids.'

'I competed in the open category, actually,' Noah said. 'But that was a while back. Once you get to the seniors, you basically have to give your whole life up to practise, and I'm more into music than shooting arrows.'

Fergal smouldered as Noah pulled a clean T-shirt on. 'Besides,' Fergal said, 'there's no point you girls getting excited when his penis doesn't work.'

'I'm an amputee, not a paraplegic,' Noah said. 'My naughty bits work just fine.'

'But you'll never get a chance to use them,' Fergal said, then, 'Oww!'

'Sack whack!' Poppy said, retreating

from a deft move in which she'd slapped Fergal between the legs with the back of her hand.

'What was that for?' Fergal said, as he lobbed the bag of frozen corn at Poppy, deliberately throwing well over her head.

'You've been treating Noah like dirt all day,' Poppy said. 'A joke's a joke, but you don't know when to stop.'

'It's what you deserve,' Suzie added.

'Sod this,' Fergal said, standing up. 'I know where I'm not welcome.'

Fergal stepped on some Lego as he headed for the front door. 'This place is a mess,' he shouted. 'Maybe you girls should do some housework instead of sitting on your fat cans watching Antiques Hunt all day.'

Joe was coming in from hosing off the wheelchair. 'What's up with old charmer?' he asked.

'Acting like a spoiled brat, as usual,' Poppy said. 'I'm sorry, Noah. You must think I'm an idiot going out with him, but he's actually quite sweet once you scratch beneath the surface.'

Suzie made a kind of grunt, indicating that she didn't agree. Noah saw that both girls were smiling at him.

'You get used to insults when you're disabled,' Noah said, feeling really happy. 'To be honest, I actually prefer people who insult me to people who treat me like I'm brain-damaged, or act overly nice just because I'm in a chair.'

He'd had an adventure, made some friends and two hot girls had told him he was buff. All things considered, Noah's day could have gone a lot worse.

6. Can't Think of A Snappy Title

It was Sunday morning. Noah sat on his bed, with a music channel on TV and the breakfast tray his mum had brought up beside him. He had 'Sexy Sadie' by The Beatles set up on his phone so that it played when she called.

'How was yesterday?' Sadie asked.

'Pretty good,' Noah said. 'Fergal was an arse the whole time.'

'What did you expect?' Sadie asked. 'How about Princess Poppy?'

'She's better than you'd think once you get to know her.'

Noah thought about mentioning the chase and hanging out at Poppy's house, but he felt bad leaving Sadie out, so he didn't want to go on about it.

'Joe's uncle e-mailed me some rough footage,' Noah said. 'There's this really cool shot of me rolling through a paddling pool. So how about you?'

'Usual boring Saturday,' Sadie said. 'Did the big supermarket shop with my dad. Took the dogs for a long walk. We're having dinner at Chiquito's this evening 'cos it's my mum's birthday in the week, but you could come round this afternoon if you want to get that history stuff out of the way.'

'Sorry, I'm rehearsing . . .'

'I was kinda thinking,' Sadie said, 'we'll never get Chris back, but we could find someone else and reboot the Unicorns if you wanted to.'

'I guess,' Noah said. 'I mean, Rock War's

a long shot.'

Noah didn't mention that Poppy and Joe had been impressed with how well he'd played and that he was hoping to get an invite to become a permanent member of Angle Grinder, even if Rock War didn't happen.

'So I hope your rehearsal works out,' Sadie said.

'Same for your Chiquito's and stuff. I need to get my arse out of bed and put some clothes on.'

'Laters, Noah.'

An hour after Sadie had called, Noah got dropped off at Joe's house by his dad. It was more like how he'd imagined one of the cool kids' houses being, with electric gates, a Mini Cooper stripped out for racing on the driveway and Fergal's drums banging inside a double garage with one door half open.

Noah had to duck slightly to get in. Lorcan was on hand and came straight over, offering to help Noah out. Fergal's right eye was almost closed, and surrounded by a massive bruise.

'I practised four of your songs at home last night,' Noah told Lorcan, and then half regretted it in case his eagerness came across as uncool.

After some fiddling about finding powerpoints for all the equipment, Angle Grinder started up playing 'Seven Nation Army' again. Then they made a fairly awful stab at Rage Against the Machine's 'Bullet in the Head'.

After that, Noah began familiarising himself with the bass line of a song Poppy had written called 'United State'. It seemed really amateurish, and he was almost relieved when a boy and a girl ducked under the garage door. Noah had never seen them before, but they were both attractive and dressed in Hollister and Ralph Lauren tops that made them fit right in with the cool set's look.

Poppy looked all excited as she ran from

her keyboard and gave the girl a hug. 'Maddy, baby! It's been ages. How's boarding school?'

'It's basically Hogwarts with sex and drugs,' Maddy explained. 'So you're not gonna believe what just happened. You know Bella?'

'Pony-tail Bella, or fat Bella?' Poppy asked.

'Pony-tail Bella,' Maddy said. 'Her dad's *minted*. They've got this massive house and she's home alone, so this whole pool-party-barbecue shindig is kicking off.'

'Cool,' Joe said. 'When?'

'Right now,' Maddy said. 'Morgan and my sister's lot are already there. There's an indoor pool and everything.'

Poppy looked around at Joe and Fergal. 'Too good to miss, right?'

Now the boy spoke. 'I already called Fastcars. They can get a seven-seater up there for fifteen pounds. That's only like two-fifty each.'

Lorcan looked a bit uneasy. 'I don't really know Bella. Do you think she'll be pissed off if I come?'

'You'll be cool,' Maddy said. 'You've been at the same parties as her hundreds of times.'

As the boy called up the taxi company to confirm the booking, Joe rushed off to find some swimming shorts.

'I'll get my dad to come and pick my drums up later,' Fergal said, as he stood beside Poppy, smiling. 'Better than an afternoon sitting in a garage.'

Poppy turned towards Noah, looking a bit awkward. 'You don't know Bella at all, do you?'

Fergal cut in, 'The only person he knows is that lesbo Sadie. Besides, there won't be room, unless we tow his chair behind us.'

A couple of minutes later, Joe came down with a few pairs of swimming shorts and a re-run of the pitying look that Poppy had given Noah.

'Sorry to bump you, Noah. But a pool party's too much to turn down. You don't mind, do you?'

Noah minded a lot, but didn't want it to

show. 'No worries,' he said curtly.

'The guitars are all rigged up,' Joe said. 'My 'rents won't mind if you want to stick around and learn some of the bass lines.'

Noah shrugged. 'I'll probably just head home.'

A horn blasted out on the driveway and Maddy led an excited posse towards a battered VW minivan. Noah got a couple of waves goodbye and a wanker gesture from Fergal as the taxi headed off the driveway and into the street.

A few moments after they left, Joe's dad came out on to his front doorstep, looking confused. 'Where'd they all go?'

Even though he was pissed off, Noah didn't want to drop Joe in it by mentioning a giant unsupervised pool party.

'They just went off to see some friend,' Noah said.

Joe's dad put his hands on his hips. 'That's just unbelievably rude. I'll be having a word when Joseph gets home.'

'It's no biggie,' Noah said. 'Really.'

'I'm happy to give you a lift home.'

'Thanks,' Noah said. 'But it's less than a mile and mostly downhill.'

'Are you sure?'

Noah didn't answer, he just let off his brake and picked up speed as he rolled down the driveway. As his chair passed low front walls and semi-detached houses, he kept thinking about the taxi stuffed with smiling teens, and imagining them all diving into a pool, drinking beer and making out with fit girls in swimsuits.

The day before he'd got a taste of being one of the cool kids and gone to bed imagining a whole new life as part of their circle. He felt like calling Sadie, but she'd just say *I told you so* and if he got back home after less than an hour his parents would ask all sorts of awkward questions too. So he just rolled slowly, feeling low and hating being stuck in a wheelchair.

7. The Court House

Thirteen Days Later

Noah felt a buzz as he entered Belfast's Court House, catching a whiff of spilled beer as he rolled past walls pasted with posters showing the music venue's glorious past: The Clash 1979, U2 May '81. The Pixies, Ramones and Green Day had all played here before hitting the big time.

This sense of history got pricked when Noah led his band into a hall that had once been the city's council chamber. The venue's mildly shabby air threw contrast on an all-new stage set, with a wall of red and orange spotlights and a giant Rock War logo. The rest of the hall had been decked out in the blue and white of the Rage Cola Corporation. Balloons, giant inflatable soft drink cans, banners. There was even a Rage Cola-branded beach buggy parked at the back of the room.

A slender woman wearing a headset with microphone dashed across as the four members of Angle Grinder glanced about, looking lost.

'Looks awesome, doesn't it?' the woman said, as she looked on a clipboard. 'I'm Amy Lott. You must be Angle Grinder.'

'That's us,' Joe agreed.

'Everyone here *loved* the video you guys put on your profile. Kinda cheeky and funny, but also the shots of Noah in the chair were quite poignant, and it was beautifully cut to the music.'

'I did some of the editing,' Joe said. 'But my uncle Toby was the brains behind it.'

Amy smiled. 'Well, your uncle is very talented! You're a few minutes early, but here's what's going to happen. First off, I'll get someone to come over and take you to make-up. Don't worry, I'm not talking about plastering you with stuff, it'll just be some foundation to stop your faces looking shiny under the stage lights. After that you'll be taken into the Rage Cola suite, and we'll film a little interview. It's nothing to stress over, we just want some footage of each band before they audition, then we'll ask you to come back and tell us how you think things went after you've played.'

'How many bands are auditioning?' Noah asked.

'How many winners?' Poppy added.

'We had a hundred and sixteen entries from Northern Ireland. We're auditioning twelve here today, and depending upon the overall standard, one to three bands from each audition will be selected for summer camp and the competition.

'Now, going back to what I was saying. After your interviews, we'll take a few still photos, then you'll film your audition, do your post-audition interview, then you'll be free to leave.'

'When will we find out if we're in or not?' Fergal asked.

'The last two auditions are being held in Newcastle and Edinburgh tomorrow. All the audition footage will be viewed on Monday, and we're hoping to announce the list of selected bands on our website either Monday, or first thing Tuesday.

'Help yourselves to drinks and sandwiches, from the table up back. And our microphones are very sensitive, so feel free to chat, but keep it down.' Then Amy backed off, with a double thumbs up and an insincere grin. 'Good luck, guys!'

As Amy jogged towards an area at the side of the stage, rigged with monitors and mixing desks, Noah followed his bandmates to the table. There was another tense quartet waiting to be interviewed, but the two bands ignored each other as Noah grabbed a can of Diet Rage and loaded nibbles on to a paper plate.

'I can't believe the judges aren't even here,' Joe said.

Noah pushed a pastry between his teeth and spoke with his mouth full. 'Rock and sausage-roll.'

It was a stupid line, but it tickled Poppy, set off a couple of kids in the other band and Noah felt good as everyone except Fergal joined the laughter. A few seconds later, a bearded man leaned out of the interview suite and shushed them.

Up on stage four serious-looking girls were plugging in their instruments. Three of the four were a bit on the chubby side, two wore glasses and they all dressed about the same, with black tees, Converse and jeans.

'Christ,' Fergal said. 'I heard Exxon signed a deal with them to pump the oil out of their zits.'

As a doddery make-up lady came over and told the other band by the food table to put their plates down and follow her, one of the girls on stage announced herself.

'Hi,' the girl said, staring down at her toes as a cameraman knelt in front of her. 'I'm Zoe, and we're Dead Cat Bounce.'

Noah almost felt sorry for Zoe as she pushed her glasses up her nose, looking about nervously while her drummer counted,

'1 – 2 – 3!'

Noah's pity turned to shock as the four girls on stage began with a heavy but beautifully played version of the theme from Mission Impossible.

Just as Noah wondered if choosing a TV theme would count against them, Dead Cat Bounce segued into 'Here Comes Your Man' by The Pixies. Zoe's vocal was high and crisp, and the band hit every mark perfectly.

Joe crouched down beside Noah and spoke over the music into his ear. 'They *really* know their stuff.'

Noah nodded. 'If all the other bands are this good, we're screwed.'

After ninety seconds of 'Here Comes Your Man', Dead Cat Bounce again segued, this time going into The Beatles' 'Revolution'.

'Why don't they play a whole song?' Fergal asked.

Noah thought he understood: the auditions could only last four minutes, and instead of sticking to a single song, Dead Cat Bounce had flexed their musical muscle and shown that they were equally adept at playing a technically tricky theme tune, a post-punk song with strong female vocals and an all-time classic.

There was no audience, but when the music stopped a few members of the Rock War crew shouted their appreciation, and gave some applause. Up on stage, the four girls were filmed as they formed a surprisingly sombre group hug, before breaking up and starting to unplug their equipment.

'They're good,' Poppy said. 'But it's flat somehow. Robotic.'

'It's not classical music,' Noah said. 'Rock music actually sounds better if it's rough around the edges.'

'Rough edges is something we've got plenty of,' Joe said, half smiling.

'All right, Angle Grinder, I've gotta make you lot pretty,' the make-up lady said, as she picked a chicken nugget off the food table. 'Follow me.'

*

The next band wasn't as talented as Dead Cat Bounce, but Noah reckoned they were at least as good as Angle Grinder. As he rolled on to stage, Noah was struggling to think of a reason why his band would get picked for Rock War over the two he'd just watched play.

Sweat seeped through the foundation on his forehead and a stage hand ran on and dabbed him down, while the cameraman got each musician to play solo for about thirty seconds. These close-up shots would be cut into the live footage if their audition made it on to TV.

Noah showboated with his bass, only for the director to tell him to play something more normal-looking.

'OK let's move this along,' the director shouted. 'We've got three more bands to film, then we've got to tear everything down and check in at the airport by eight.'

'Quiet please,' the assistant director shouted. 'Lighting is sequenced.'

'Camera rolling.'

'Sound rolling.'

'In your own time,' the director said. 'Action!'

Poppy took a half step up to the microphone, gave one of her million-dollar smiles and sounded completely unflustered.

'Hey! We're Angle Grinder, and this is our version of "Peaches" by The Stranglers.'

Noah played the intro riff on bass. Poppy had her keyboard set up to sound like a vintage Hammond organ and Joe's slightly gruff Belfast accent suited the lyrics. They'd practised the song a hundred times, but Noah felt like his body was in a vice.

As his strings reverberated around the Court House's giant PA system, Noah tried to ignore the director giving hand signals to her crew, the camera moving on rails in front of the stage and the computer-controlled lights flashing and swivelling overhead.

For some reason, Noah's brain fixated on the abuse he'd get from Fergal if he messed up. But for all his angst, the quartet got to the end of the song without messing up. Noah made a huge relieved gasp as silence broke out.

'And cut!' the director shouted. 'Is everyone happy with the footage? Sound? Great! Thanks, kids, you're free to go.'

8. F5

Noah tried to act like it was no big deal, but he didn't sleep on Saturday night. On Sunday morning, he got the Rock War site up on his laptop, read through all the cool stuff about the summer camp. Then he spent half an hour watching videos on the profiles of some of the other bands in the Belfast audition.

If he were the judge, Noah reckoned he'd pick Dead Cat Bounce, because they were the best musicians. But he wondered if the real judges would go for looks over talent, in which case he reckoned Angle Grinder had a chance, because the three boys in the band were OK-looking and Poppy was stunning.

Noah told Sadie that he couldn't see how Angle Grinder would get in when she came round on Sunday afternoon to do the history project.

Noah loaded the Rock War site on to his phone before school on Monday, navigating to the page that tantalised him with: *The auditions are now complete and the twelve bands selected for Rock War will be announced on this page soon!*

Noah refreshed the page on the bus and again as he headed through school gates.

'Touch anxious, are we?' Sadie teased, as they sat next to each other in morning registration.

Sadie mocked Noah's posture, stooped anxiously over his iPhone.

'I can never get a data signal in this part of the school,' Noah moaned.

'Put the phone away before I take it away,

Noah,' Mr Hammond warned.

Noah sneaked his phone out again at morning break and finally got the Rock War page to refresh, after ten minutes sitting in the school's front yard faffing about.

'Still nowt,' he moaned.

'You sure don't look like someone who says it's no big deal,' Sadie said. 'You're all jittery, like you drank twenty coffees or something.'

Noah replied defensively. 'Well, I obviously wouldn't have entered if I didn't want to get in, would I? I don't know why you're so down on it. I mean, what'll you do this summer? Sit at home reading and surfing the web. Maybe a couple of weeks in France or something.'

Sadie smiled. 'I just think those TV talent shows are cheesy crap. But I guess the summer training academy might be a giggle.'

'Did you mean what you said about getting the Unicorns back together?' Noah asked.

Sadie nodded. 'I'll ask around, see who's interested.'

'We could put up a notice on the board in the music room,' Noah suggested, but Sadie shook her head.

'I've heard about people who've done that,' she said. 'You just attract a bunch of freaks. Like, little year sevens who can barely play and stuff. And then they all get pissy when you reject them.'

Noah and Sadie had fifty minutes of history before lunch. They usually went straight to the canteen afterwards, but Noah headed in the opposite direction.

'I can get a better signal over that side of the building,' Noah explained. 'Plus, Joe or Poppy might have heard something.'

'I'll leave you to it,' Sadie said. 'I'm starving, and I can do without the moron calling me a lesbian for the 5,000th time.'

'It'll take two minutes,' Noah said. 'You'll probably get to eat sooner because you can use the staff counter if you're with me.'

'True,' Sadie said.

She pushed Noah part of the way, because he was trying to refresh the Rock War page. They got some *you don't belong here* looks as they headed out towards the edge of the all-weather pitches. Lorcan, Poppy, Joe and the rest of the year nine cool set were standing around eating bags of chips.

'Chip?' Joe asked, as he tilted his bag towards Noah.

'Where'd you get them?' Sadie asked, as she and Noah each took a couple of Joe's chips.

'Chippy across the ways,' Joe said, pointing beyond the school fence. 'You just hop over the low wall, behind the gym. Teachers on lunch duty don't want hassle. So they turn a blind eye as long as you don't do it blatantly in front of them.'

'Good chips,' Noah said. 'The data connection on my phone sucks. Have you heard anything?'

Joe looked at Poppy. 'I thought you were

gonna text him.'

Poppy shook her head. 'You said . . .'

Joe waved his hand in front of his face. 'Doesn't matter. They've still not put the full list up on the website, but Poppy got an e-mail. *Thanks for taking part, it was a close-run thing, but we're sorry to say Angle Grinder has not been selected for Rock War.*

'Well, that sucks,' Noah said, as his body slumped. 'At least we gave it a shot.'

Sadie quite liked the fact that Noah wouldn't be off at the Rock War training camp all summer, but tried to hide her relief. Fergal made a kind of flicking gesture with his hand.

'So Lorcan's back in the band and you're out, loser,' Fergal said. 'Now sling your hook. Go hang out front with the geeks, talking about Minecraft and the new Star Wars.'

Noah hoped Joe or Poppy would say something about him possibly staying in the band, but they kept quiet, while several other kids from their group laughed approvingly. Up to this point Noah had sucked up the abuse in the interest of band harmony. But he wasn't in the band any more so he wheeled forward quickly.

'What?' Fergal taunted. 'You gonna beat me up, turd?'

Noah flicked his left arm up, batting the chip packet out of Fergal's hand. A collective gasp went up as half a pack of ketchup-smeared chips pelted the floor.

'You're just a thicko,' Noah spat. 'And these guys suck up to you because you're hard. But behind your back, they all take the piss because you're soooo stupid.'

Fergal stepped forwards, wagging his finger. 'You're lucky you're in that wheelchair. If you weren't I'd be kicking you from one end of this playground to the other right now.'

'Go for it,' Noah taunted, bunching fists and raising his muscular arms.

As Fergal stepped up to Noah's chair,

looking furious, Sadie grabbed the handles on the back and pulled Noah half a metre out.

'Hey,' Noah said, glancing furiously back at Sadie. 'You've got no right.'

Noah reached down and flipped on his brake. But Sadie had been pushing Noah around since they were little. She knew that the brake acted on the front wheels, and overrode it by tilting the chair backwards. At the same time, Joe and a couple of other lads got in front of Fergal.

'The little freak's not worth getting expelled over,' Lorcan said.

This comment hurt Noah more than anything Fergal had ever said, because up to this point Lorcan had been really friendly.

'Stop my chair,' Noah demanded. 'I wanna have this out with him.'

'He'll beat the hell out of you,' Sadie warned, as she stopped pushing the chair and made a theatrical scowl back towards Fergal. 'You knocked his chips on the ground and dissed him in front of his crew. Why not quit while you're ahead?'

Sadie let go of the chair. Noah took his brake off, and stared at Fergal before giving his head a little shake and raising his hands.

'You're right,' he told Sadie dejectedly.

'I'm always right,' Sadie said, as Noah decided that it was best to leave hastily, in case Fergal broke loose. 'You should know that by now.'

9. Outta the Blue

Noah was gutted about Rock War, but at least the awkwardness it had caused with Sadie was behind them. He had dinner at Sadie's house and was still bloated from her dad's fish pie when he got home. He stripped off, shaved the few flakes of stubble that passed for his beard and manoeuvred himself from his chair on to a shower seat.

As Noah rolled back to his bedroom, wearing night shorts and an AC/DC T-shirt, he heard his mobile ringing. After fishing it out of his school trousers, he answered casually with, 'Hey,' because the only people who ever called him were Sadie and a couple of his cousins.

'Noah Crook?' a man asked, as Noah towelled damp hair with his free hand.

'Speaking,' Noah said. 'Who is this?'

'I missed your audition on Saturday,' the man said, firing words at a hundred miles per hour. 'I was directing the other audition over in Birmingham. My name's Zig Allen, I'm the producer for Rock War.'

Noah sounded surprised. 'How'd you get my number? It was Poppy who submitted the Angle Grinder profile.'

'You didn't make your Unicorns profile public,' Zig explained, 'but you did save and upload quite a few details, which are still on our server. You're an impressive lead guitar player, so it almost seemed like a waste having you play bass for Angle Grinder.'

'The Unicorns didn't pan out,' Noah said. 'We only had three members, and two of them weren't particularly serious about it.'

'Angle Grinder are an OK band,' Zig said. 'But Dead Cat Bounce had more of the qualities that we're looking for.'

'I'm glad they made it. Those girls are seriously talented.'

'They're superb,' Zig agreed. 'But you know what, Noah? Reality TV isn't about who's the best musician. If I just wanted that, we'd just recruit kids from all the best music schools.'

'So what is it about?' Noah asked.

'Stories,' Zig said exuberantly. 'A fat woman in a frumpy dress, sings like an angel and becomes a megastar. A weird Korean rapper does a silly dance and gets two billion hits on YouTube. Dead Cat Bounce has a story. It goes like this: four shy-but-brilliant geeks form a band. We get a dermatologist to sort their skin, replace their glasses with contacts, slap on some make-up and cool clothes and BOOM, you have a story.'

'Ugly ducklings turned to handsome princesses,' Noah said.

'You got it, kid. So far we've picked nine bands for Rock War, and they've all got a story. There's some Christian kids who sing about Jesus, a girl from Dudley who lives in a dingy flat and looks after her sick nan. There's two bands from London who hate each other's guts so much that their mums got arrested for brawling in the street. Angle Grinder was three average musicians, who got someone to make a cool video for their profile. But you . . .'

Noah saw what Zig was getting at and was mildly offended. 'I'm in a wheelchair, so I've got a story to tell.'

'No flies on you,' Zig said, laughing. 'But think about it this way, Noah. All your life, there's been things you can't do because of that wheelchair, now for once it's giving you a leg-up. If you'll excuse the phrase.'

'So where do I fit in?' Noah asked. 'How can you want me, but not the rest of my band?'

'There was a band at the Newcastle audition called Frosty Vader. Two cousins who are kinda crazy. They write music that's more electronica than rock. Weird sound effects. They go on stage dressed in orange prison suits, they throw firecrackers at one another and do some little parkour moves. But don't get me wrong, this isn't a novelty act. They're a bit all over the place, but they're really talented.'

'They must have had four members to audition though.'

'Obviously,' Zig agreed. 'They had a guitar player and drummer, but they were plodders, making up the numbers. A player with your kind of talent would be able to make a much bigger contribution to the group.'

'What about the fourth member?' Noah asked.

'If you've got any thoughts, I'm all ears,' Zig said. 'Possibly one of your bandmates? The other three members of Angle Grinder all looked good. Maybe the girl, Pippa?'

'Poppy,' Noah corrected. 'If you're looking for a girl, there's my friend Sadie. You might have seen her in the Unicorns video I uploaded.'

'Short hair, boyish?'

'That's her.'

'Is she a lesbian?'

'No,' Noah said.

'Pity,' Zig said. 'Two crazy cousins, a kid in a wheelchair and a fourteen-year-old lesbian would almost have been TV heaven.'

'But she's really important to me,' Noah explained. 'Like, you're looking for good stories. Well, Sadie's been my best friend since I was little. We've always done everything together, and she's kind of like my bodyguard.'

'Hmm,' Zig said. 'Let me chew on that. I might have to meet this Sadie.'

'What about the three judges?' Noah said. 'Don't they have final say over which bands get in?'

Zig laughed. 'I am the judges right now.'

'What do you mean?'

'Noah, when this show goes on air, there will be footage from the Belfast audition. It will be edited to show the three judges in situ, and there will be a heated discussion about how they eventually come to pick Dead Cat Bounce. But right now, we're still in negotiation with a number of agents over who the Rock War judges will actually be.'

'So the judges don't really pick?'

Zig sounded horrified. 'You can't *seriously* expect the success of a multi-million-pound TV project to depend on the decisions of some random celebrities.'

'Isn't that cheating?' Noah asked.

'Once the show goes live and the press stick their noses in, you have to go by the book,' Zig explained. 'But there's a lot more leeway when a show is only in pre-production.'

'Right,' Noah said, feeling rather naive.

'So I'm gonna speak to a few more people about this in the morning. But in principle, would you be happy to fly over to Newcastle and meet with Frosty Vader?'

Noah still felt guilty about abandoning Sadie to join Rock War and decided to take a chance. 'Being in a wheelchair isn't easy,' he said, adopting his most earnest tone. 'So I'd only feel comfortable doing the summer camp thing with my friend Sadie. Otherwise I'm out.'

Zig laughed. 'So you're making demands now, Noah? I like you, you've got a brain on your shoulders. I've got to make some more calls before this is finalised, but we've got to announce the full list of bands by midnight tomorrow.'

'Cool. What about my parents?'

'Text me their number after you hang up,' Zig said. 'Then I'll have my people call your people first thing tomorrow morning. Goodnight.'

'Night,' Noah said, but Zig Allen was already dialling his next call.

10. Integrity

Noah didn't call Sadie because he wanted to tell her face to face and blow her away.

'. . . So Zig's PA spoke to my parents late last night. Then this morning Zig calls again, he couldn't make arrangements for me to fly with a wheelchair at short notice, so the two cousins from Frosty Vader are being taken out of school early. They're getting a 4 p.m. flight from Newcastle. There's a taxi picking us up from my house and we're all meeting up at some hotel near the airport at six.'

Sadie looked a bit confused. 'What, for a jam session?'

Noah shrugged. 'Maybe, but I think it's probably just a meeting.'

'It's so bogus,' Sadie said sourly, as they rounded a corner, heading towards their bus stop.

'What's bogus?'

'The whole thing's set up,' Sadie explained. Which just confirms everything I've ever thought about trash TV talent shows.'

Noah looked confused. 'Zig seemed OK on the phone.'

Sadie tutted. 'Faked auditions, non-existent judges. Taking the most interesting members from two bands who don't even live on the same side of the Irish Sea.'

'It's entertainment,' Noah shrugged. 'We're not talking about rigging a general election. It's just bending the truth a little to make a fun TV show.'

'Haven't you got one grain of integrity?'

Sadie asked indignantly. 'This Zig Allen creep openly admits that he wants you in the show not because of your talent, but because you're in a wheelchair. How on earth can you stomach that?'

'Give us a break,' Noah moaned. 'It's a bit of fun. Why have you always got to be so high and mighty about everything?'

They'd now walked close enough to the bus stop for other kids from their school to overhear.

'I've never seen you like this,' Sadie said. 'I thought you had a bit of backbone. If you want to be a performing monkey on some Saturday night TV show, go right ahead. Just don't say I didn't warn you when you end up making a colossal tit of yourself.'

'All my life there's been a million things I can't do,' Noah spat, as he thumped the arms of his chair. 'So if I catch a break because I'm in a wheelchair, I'm not gonna complain.'

'Fine,' Sadie said, folding her arms as they

reached the stop. 'I've got nothing more to say on the matter.'

'I'll ask someone else to audition with me,' Noah said. 'See if I care.'

Sadie half turned away, sulking. When the bus arrived a couple of minutes later, Noah took his usual route up a retractable ramp and into the disabled space, while Sadie stomped upstairs.

Noah felt a bit sad. He really liked the fact that Sadie was quirky and principled, but sometimes that also made her a stubborn pain in the arse.

The bus was full of rowdy kids, so he left his phone in his pocket until he got off close to school. As Sadie strode purposefully through the school gates, Noah rolled to a halt outside and wondered how to replace her. Seeing as Frosty Vader had already auditioned with four members, Noah reckoned it wasn't critical that he bring a second person along to the meeting, but he much preferred the idea of going to the

Rock War summer camp with at least one person he knew.

Joe seemed like the only option. His playing was average, but Joe was easy to get along with when he wasn't hanging with Fergal and the rest of that crowd and Noah suspected Zig would like the fact that he was good-looking in a shaggy-haired kind of way.

Noah tried ringing, but Joe's phone went to voicemail, so he sent a text and got a reply as he puffed his way up the stupidly steep ramp leading to his school's main entrance.

*

Periods one and two were awkward. Noah and Sadie always sat together, and things remained frosty, with clipped sentences exchanged over a shared geography textbook.

At morning break, Noah wheeled to the back of the school where he'd arranged to meet Joe, to flesh out the text exchange they'd had before registration. Joe stayed close to the school building so that Noah didn't have to go far, but when Noah approached he was annoyed to see Fergal standing there as well.

'Loser!' Fergal said.

Joe started speaking as Noah gave him a *why the hell is Fergal here* look. 'I've got a contact lens appointment after school,' Joe said apologetically. 'I called my ma up to try and get her to change it, but she's leaving work early so she can be there with her credit card. And she's booked three weeks in Spain for summer hols, so she was never really down with the Rock War thing anyway.'

'Oh,' Noah said weakly. 'Pity.'

'The good news is, I'm free,' Fergal said. 'So what time's this car picking us up?'

Noah practically swallowed his tongue. 'I'm pretty sure they don't want a drummer,' he blurted. 'Frosty Vader play some kind of electronica, so I think they use a drum machine.'

'I play guitar as well,' Fergal said.

Joe nodded. 'He's as good as me.'

'I don't know,' Noah said. 'I just don't think you're what Zig's looking for.'

Fergal shrugged. 'We'll see when we get there.'

'But . . .' Noah stammered.

Fergal squatted down so that he was on Noah's level, and cracked his knuckles. 'Sounds like you're making excuses,' he said darkly. 'Anyone would think you don't like me, or something.'

Noah pushed his chair back half a turn and took a deep breath. 'I *don't* like you,' he said, unable to hide his nerves completely. 'You treat me like dirt and constantly insult my best friend.'

Fergal darted behind Noah's chair, shoved it forwards so that he was pinned against a chain link fence and then yanked his ear.

'You're lucky I didn't smash your face in yesterday,' Fergal said menacingly. 'But if you ruin my chance on this, I'll make your life a living hell.'

To emphasise his point, Fergal rammed the wheelchair hard into the fence.

Noah looked furiously at Joe. 'You're a decent guy. How come you let him act like this?'

Joe seemed stung by the rebuke, but backed off like it wasn't his problem.

'I live at 29B, Castledene Grove,' Fergal said, as he patted Noah's cheek. 'Text me when you know what time the car's picking me up.'

As Fergal backed up, he looked around at Joe. 'What's your problem?' Fergal asked.

Much to Noah's disgust, Joe shrugged, then grinned and said. 'No problem, buddy.'

11. Drive of Your Life

Sadie lived in a little Victorian terrace, decked out new-agey style with lots of rattan furniture, wind chimes and shabby Indian rugs. Both parents worked, so she was surprised to come home and find her mum with medical notes spread all over the dining table.

'You're early,' Sadie noted, as she took a bottle of freshly squeezed out of the fridge.

'I had a meeting in town, and it seemed a bit pointless going back to the office for an hour.'

'Juice?' Sadie asked.

Her mum shook her head. 'So how was your day, sweetie?'

'Meh,' Sadie said. 'Noah pissed me off. He's got a chance to get into this Rock War thing by the back door. And he's like all up for it, even though they blatantly only want him because he's in a wheelchair.'

'Sometimes you have to take opportunities in life, however they present themselves.'

Sadie looked a little cross. 'But he's a total sell-out. I told him I'm having nothing to do with it.'

Sadie's mum smiled. 'So are you talking to him? Or are you two having another tiff?'

'We're kinda talking.'

'And it's up to Noah, surely. If you go through life expecting to agree with everything your friends do, you'll end up with a very short list of friends.'

This struck a raw nerve, because Noah was basically Sadie's only friend. 'Why are you taking his side?' she said irritably. 'I'm not doing it, anyway.'

Sadie's mum sat up straight, and took off her reading glasses. 'So you could have got in too?'

'I'm not a sell-out,' Sadie said firmly. 'Unlike certain people.'

Her mum couldn't help but smile. 'You're so stubborn. This could be an incredible opportunity for you. You'd meet lots of new people. Learn lots about music and the media. And you know money's tight with your dad only on twenty hours. We might book a week's camping in France or something, but the other five weeks of summer holidays you'll just be stuck in the house.'

'I guess,' Sadie said reluctantly. 'But he'll have got someone else on board by now. Joe or Poppy I expect.'

'Did Noah say that?'

Sadie shrugged. 'Noah didn't say anything. He came back from morning break in a really bad mood. We sat together in a couple of lessons, but he hardly said a word.'

'So maybe he didn't get someone,' Sadie's mum suggested.

'Even if he didn't, I'm not gonna ring him now and beg after I told him he was a sell-out.'

Sadie's mum laughed. 'You're so black and white. You don't *have* to ring Noah and beg. Just ring up, ask if he got someone. If he did, you say *that's great* and wish him luck.'

'But . . .' Sadie said, screwing up her face and not wanting to admit that her mum was probably right.

Now Sadie's mum spoke more firmly. 'Go upstairs and call Noah. You might regret it for the rest of your life if you don't.'

*

Noah's mum was excited, and got a thrill when a big Mercedes limo pulled up outside their house.

'Oooh, you're a proper little star!' she

said, as she gave her son a kiss. 'I hope it all goes well.'

Noah had started the day in a great mood, but now the whole thing was ruined. Not getting into Rock War after coming so close would suck, but the idea of six weeks living with Fergal was even worse. They set off once the driver had put Noah's wheelchair in the boot.

'Mr Allen says that the boys you're meeting have to be on a 9 p.m. flight back to Newcastle,' the driver told Noah politely. 'Traffic going out the airport can be hell at this time of day, so will you mind giving your friend a call and telling him to be ready when I arrive?'

Noah did what he'd been asked, but Fergal's voice on the other end of the phone filled him with dread. Fergal lived on the same dodgy estate as Poppy and the big Merc was going down her street as Noah saw Sadie's name flashing on his iPhone.

'Hey,' he said warily.

'How's it going?' Sadie asked.

'Good,' Noah lied. 'Really good.'

'I just wanted to say I'm sorry about this morning,' Sadie said. 'Did you get someone to fill in?'

Noah was too embarrassed to admit that Joe had turned out to be a dick and that he'd got lumbered with Fergal under threat of violence.

'Kinda,' Noah said weakly.

'What does that mean?' Sadie asked. 'Only, I know I got on my high horse a bit earlier, but my family's not doing anything much this summer and the Rock War training camp does sound pretty cool.'

The Mercedes looked thoroughly out of place as it took a right into a dead-end street. There were lads on bikes circling a burned-out Toyota and a long wall, saturated with graffiti. Fergal stood by a gate, dressed in jeans and his best Hollister polo shirt.

'Hang on, Sadie,' Noah said. 'I'll call you back.'

Noah's brain churned, at once tantalised by the prospect of the coolest summer ever with his best friend, but terrified by what Fergal might do if he stood him up. As the driver started slowing down, Noah made a snap decision and thumped on the headrest.

'That was my mate,' he blurted. 'I'm really sorry, but I got the wrong address. She lives with her dad one week and her mum the next. We need to get to Springfield Avenue.'

The driver looked a bit peeved, but he stopped a couple of houses shy of Fergal's front gate and began reversing out of the cul-de-sac. As the driver stopped to programme Sadie's address into his sat nav, Fergal started a brisk walk towards the car. The driver caught sight and looked wary.

'Do you know him?' he asked.

'Never seen him before in my life,' Noah said.

As Fergal got to within a couple of metres of the car, the driver gave up on programming the sat nav and started reversing out.

'Hey,' Fergal shouted. 'Where you going?'

Fergal managed to smack one hand against the bonnet, then he stumbled in a pothole as the big car picked up speed and reversed into the main road.

'Don't like the look of him,' the driver noted, as he roared away. 'Don't much like taking a car into an estate like this full stop.'

Noah took a last glance through the side window, seeing Fergal in the middle of the road, steaming mad.

12. Cal & Otis

Calvin and Otis Gregg were cousins, but they'd often get mistaken for twins. Cal was thirteen, tiny nose, cropped blond hair. Otis was fourteen, stockier and shorter. Zig Allen had a cameraman shooting as the pair met up with Sadie and Noah, shaking hands, and introducing one another in a clash of Belfast and Newcastle accents.

After the hellos things got a bit awkward.

'I assume everyone's hungry?' Zig said, breaking the silence.

The four band members, Cal's mum, Zig,

the cameraman and Zig's PA followed Zig across the hotel lobby and took a big table in a near-empty restaurant. Noah sat at the end, next to Otis. He didn't know what to say at first, but Otis said that Zig had sent him a video of Noah playing solo and had been impressed by it.

After that, the pair got comfortable, talking about the kind of music they liked. A few chairs down, Sadie seemed to be getting along just as well with Cal. After a gourmet burger and a slab of choc-chip cheesecake, Noah felt cheerful and a touch bloated as they headed back into the lobby.

As the cameraman led the way, Noah listened in as Zig explained to Otis' mum about how the embryonic band could rehearse together over half-term week and most weekends over the eight weeks before summer holidays and the start of the Rock War academy.

Zig had booked one of the hotel's meeting rooms, and they passed through its double doors to find that a director and a hot female presenter had tilted the meeting table back against the wall, and set up a mini studio with two lighting panels and a green screen background.

Noah, Sadie, Cal and Otis were each given T-shirts with the Rock War logo on, and told to stand in front of the green screen.

'I'm just recording some sound-bites,' the director explained. 'First, I want all four of you to say, 'We're Frosty Vader and we're gonna win Rock War!'

Noah wore a huge grin as he lined up with the centre of the green screen, with Sadie down on one knee beside him and Cal and Otis behind. It seemed weird predicting victory for a band that had yet to play a single note together, but the prospect of spending summer training to be a rock star with his best friend alongside was a massive buzz.

'We're Frosty Vader and we're gonna . . .

tits! What was I supposed to say?' Sadie asked, before cracking up laughing.

Everyone joined the laughter as the director made a circling motion and said. 'Keep rolling, do it again.'

The second attempt worked fine, and the director recorded a third to be on the safe side.

'OK,' she said. 'Now I want to interview each of your individually. Just three or four questions, telling us a little bit about yourselves and what it feels like to be selected for Rock War.'

As the presenter faffed with her hair, Noah wheeled up to Zig. 'Can I use the toilet while you record the others?'

Sadie needed to go as well and the pair found ladies and disabled toilets at the end of a short hallway, just beyond the hotel's reception desk. After hunting for a light switch, Noah was pleased to find himself in a large and immaculately clean disabled cubicle. But as he flicked the lock on the door, he saw something move behind him.

'I thought you'd end up in here,' Fergal said, as he stepped forward. 'I warned you, didn't I?'

Before Noah got a chance to reply, Fergal slapped him hard across the cheek. Noah backed up towards the door, but as he reached to undo the lock, Fergal batted his hand away.

'Sadie,' Noah shouted desperately, as he backed up towards the wall beside the toilet.

'Did you think you could get away with it because you're in the chair?' Fergal asked, as he closed in with his fists bunched.

Noah ducked, so Fergal's punch only glanced the top of his head. Realising that backing into a corner wasn't a good strategy, Noah charged forwards with his head down. As Fergal thumped him in the back, Noah got his muscular arms around Fergal's waist and squeezed.

Fergal gave Noah a couple more slaps in the back, then tried to break loose, putting his hands on Noah's shoulders and trying to spread his interlocked fingers.

'What the . . .' Sadie asked herself, as she exited the ladies and heard thumping and gasps coming from the disabled cubicle.

As Noah's knuckles turned white, Fergal brought his knee up, slugging him in the gut. Badly winded, Noah lost the strength to keep his hands around Fergal's waist, and Fergal's other knee caught him painfully across the bridge of his nose. Unable to move, or breathe, Noah backed up to the wall beside the toilet, totally at Fergal's mercy.

Outside, Sadie saw that like most disabled toilets, the door had a simple lock that could be over-ridden. She fumbled in her jeans, came out with a 50p coin and used it to turn the giant screw head beneath the door handle.

Noah had his arms up shielding his face as Sadie charged in. Catching Fergal by surprise, she knocked him sideways, he hit the toilet and rolled off at the other side. As he staggered to his feet, Sadie picked up a metal waste bin, which made a very satisfying thud when she thrust it as hard as she could against the back of Fergal's head.

'I'll kill both of you,' Fergal roared.

He glanced from side to side, unsure who to attack first. Sadie opened the door wide, and Noah went for the exit. He wheeled down the short corridor and into the hotel lobby, yelling, 'Someone help us!'

Sadie tried to follow Noah out of the cubicle, but Fergal charged, butting her in the stomach, lifting her feet off the ground and slamming her painfully against a mirrored back wall. After dodging a couple of wild punches, Sadie made another scramble for the door, just as Zig Allen and a hotel porter charged into the cubicle.

The porter was a huge red-faced man, who yanked Fergal backwards, knocked him against the wall, then tried to bring him down, dragging him by his shirt collar. Fergal ended up sprawled out just in front of Sadie, with a giant tear in his precious Hollister polo. She wasn't usually mean, but Fergal's hand flat on the floor was too good to resist and she stamped down with the heel of her boot.

'Yeowww!' Fergal screamed.

Before Sadie could do anything else, Zig grabbed ahold and pulled her backwards out of the cubicle. She met up with Noah and a crowd of onlookers in the lobby. As Sadie straightened her bra and jeans, a guy at reception was calling the police, while a waiter from the restaurant handed Noah a big wodge of napkins to deal with a bloody nose.

'She stole my place,' Fergal spat, as he stood in the cubicle doorway, clutching his hand and blocked in by the bulky porter. 'I'll have all of you. You wait! You wait and see.'

Sadie looked at Noah. 'Why's he here?' she asked.

Noah had been too embarrassed to tell Sadie that he'd been railroaded into bringing Fergal before she'd changed her mind about being in Rock War, and there hadn't been a chance to explain since.

'It's complicated,' Noah said, as he looked around and saw that the cameraman was now in the middle of the lobby, filming the chaos.

The cameraman and the female presenter closed in on Noah.

'What just happened?' the presenter asked, sticking a microphone in his face.

As Noah took the bloody tissues from his nose, there was a blue flash from a cop car pulling up outside.

'Noah, are you OK?' the presenter asked, crouching beside Noah's chair and looking earnestly into the camera.

'Just some crazy guy attacked me in the toilet,' Noah gasped. 'No idea what it's all about.'

The cameraman swung away from Noah's

chair as two female cops rushed in. After a brief conversation with the hotel manager, they relieved the porter of his job barricading Fergal into the disabled toilet.

'I should be on Rock War,' Fergal screamed, pointing at Sadie as he fought the two cops trying to put him in cuffs. 'I got screwed over. You're dead. You're all dead.'

The cameraman wasn't sure if any of this footage could be used in the TV show, but he was certain Zig Allen would blast him if he didn't get it. Seeing Noah, sitting in his chair with blood smeared over his top lip and dripping on to his Rock War T-shirt, the cameraman gestured towards the presenter.

'Noah,' the presenter said. 'What we just witnessed shows just how desperate a lot of people are to get into Rock War. Are you feeling OK?'

'Just a bloody nose,' Noah said, half smiling. 'I reckon I'll live.'

'And it's not put you off? You're still

looking forward to the Rock War academy and Frosty Vader getting a shot at the big-time?'

'For sure,' Noah said, as another drip of blood ran off his chin. 'Rock War's gonna be amazing!'

Meet Jay.
Summer.
And Dylan.

OUT FEB 2014

Jay plays guitar, writes songs and dreams of being a rock star. But his ambitions are stifled by seven siblings and a terrible drummer.

Summer works hard at school, looks after her nan and has a one-in-a-million singing voice. But can her talent triumph over her nerves?

Dylan is happiest lying on his bunk smoking, but his school rugby coach has other ideas, and Dylan reluctantly joins a band to avoid crunching tackles and icy mud.

They're about to enter the biggest battle of their lives. And there's everything to play for.

Also available as an ebook

www.rockwar.com

Hodder Children's Books

CHERUB ™

THE RECRUIT
Robert Muchamore

A terrorist doesn't let strangers in her flat because they might be undercover police or intelligence agents, but her children bring their mates home and they run all over the place. The terrorist doesn't know that one of these kids has bugged every room in her house, made copies of all her computer files and stolen her address book. The kid works for CHERUB.

CHERUB agents are aged between ten and seventeen. They live in the real world, slipping under adult radar and getting information that sends criminals and terrorists to jail.

For official purposes, these children do not exist.

www.cherubcampus.com

Hodder
Children's
Books

CHERUB ™

PEOPLE'S REPUBLIC
Robert Muchamore

Twelve-year-old Ryan is CHERUB's newest recruit. He's got his first mission: infiltrating the billion-dollar Aramov criminal empire. But he's got no idea that this routine job will lead him into an explosive adventure involving drug smugglers, illegal immigrants and human trafficking, or that his first mission will turn into one of the biggest in CHERUB's history.

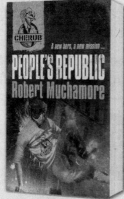

OUT NOW

Also available as an ebook

www.cherubcampus.com

Hodder Children's Books

WORLD **BOOK** DAY *fest*

6 MARCH 2014

Want to **READ** more?

Visit your **LOCAL BOOKSHOP**

- Get some great recommendations for what to read next

- Meet your favourite authors & illustrators at brilliant events

- Discover books you never even knew existed!

WWW.BOOKSELLERS.ORG.UK/ BOOKSHOPSEARCH

Join your **LOCAL LIBRARY**

You can browse and borrow from a HUGE selection of books and get recommendations of what to read next from expert librarians—all for FREE! You can also discover libraries' wonderful children's and family reading activities.

WWW.FINDALIBRARY.CO.UK

GET ONLINE! Visit **WWW.WORLDBOOKDAY.COM** to discover a whole *new* world of books!

- Downloads and activities
- Cool games, trailers and videos
- Author events in your area
- News, competitions and new books —all in a **FREE** monthly email